Dear Parent:
Your child's love of reading starts here!

Every child learns to read in a different way and at his or her own speed. Some go back and forth between reading levels and read favorite books again and again. Others read through each level in order. You can help your young reader improve and become more confident by encouraging his or her own interests and abilities. From books your child reads with you to the first books he or she reads alone, there are I Can Read Books for every stage of reading:

SHARED READING
Basic language, word repetition, and whimsical illustrations, ideal for sharing with your emergent reader

BEGINNING READING
Short sentences, familiar words, and simple concepts for children eager to read on their own

READING WITH HELP
Engaging stories, longer sentences, and language play for developing readers

READING ALONE
Complex plots, challenging vocabulary, and high-interest topics for the independent reader

ADVANCED READING
Short paragraphs, chapters, and exciting themes for the perfect bridge to chapter books

I Can Read Books have introduced children to the joy of reading since 1957. Featuring award-winning authors and illustrators and a fabulous cast of beloved characters, I Can Read Books set the standard for beginning readers.

A lifetime of discovery begins with the magical words "I Can Read!"

Visit www.icanread.com for information
on enriching your child's reading experience.

Back in the Saddle

*For every rider who has
ever taken a spill. (That
includes both of us!)
—C.H. and A.K.*

I Can Read Book® is a trademark of HarperCollins Publishers.

Pony Scouts: Back in the Saddle. Copyright © 2011 by HarperCollins Publishers. All rights reserved. Manufactured in China. No part of this book may be used or reproduced in any manner whatsoever without written permission except in the case of brief quotations embodied in critical articles and reviews. For information address HarperCollins Children's Books, a division of HarperCollins Publishers, 10 East 53rd Street, New York, NY 10022.
www.icanread.com

Library of Congress catalog card number: 2010021961
ISBN 978-0-06-125539-7 (trade bdg.) ISBN 978-0-06-125541-0 (pbk.)

11 12 13 14 15 SCP 10 9 8 7 6 5 4 3 2 1   ❖   First Edition

I Can Read!

READING 2 WITH HELP

PONY SCOUTS

Back in the Saddle

Splash

by Catherine Hapka
pictures by Anne Kennedy

HARPER

An Imprint of HarperCollinsPublishers

Annie couldn't wait for school to end.
Today she was going home
with her friend Jill.
Jill lived on a pony farm!

Their friend Meg came, too.

The three girls called themselves

the Pony Scouts.

"Ready to ride?" Jill asked

when they got to the barn.

"Just a second," Annie said.

She hung up a drawing of a cute foal
on the Pony Scouts bulletin board.

"It's a picture of Surprise.

She's one month old today!"
Annie said.

"You should know, Annie,"

Meg said with a laugh.

"You're the one who found Surprise!"

Surprise got her name because
nobody knew that her mother, Rosy,
was going to have a foal.

"Where are Surprise and Rosy now?"

Annie asked.

"Mom put them out in the field.

We can visit them after our lesson

and sing 'Happy Birthday,'" Jill said.

Today Annie was riding

a gentle pony named Splash.

She got him ready

and led him out to the riding ring.

Surprise and Rosy
were grazing in the next field.
"I can't wait until
Surprise is old enough to ride,"
Annie told her friends.

Soon the lesson started.

Jill's mom asked the girls

to let go of their reins.

She showed them how to move

their arms like windmills.

"This will help your balance,"
said Jill's mom.
"It's fun!" Meg cried.

15

Annie was having fun, too.

But being a windmill on horseback

was harder than it looked!

Once she almost lost her balance.

But then she caught herself.

Whew!

After a while Jill's mom
had them try the windmills
at a trot.
That was even harder!

Just then Annie noticed Surprise
bucking and playing in the field.
She turned to watch the foal
and felt herself slip to the side.

This time, Annie

couldn't keep her balance.

She fell off and landed on her rear!

"Ouch!" she cried.

Splash stopped and looked at her.

"Annie!" Jill and Meg cried.

Jill's mom rushed over.

"Are you okay?" she asked.

Annie wanted to cry.

She wasn't hurt.

But falling off was scary!

"I think I'm okay," she said.

"Do you want to get back on?"

Jill's mom asked.

Annie wasn't sure.

"Maybe I should wait

until next time," she whispered.

Jill looked worried.

"Are you sure?" she asked.

"If you wait, you might be
even more scared next time."

Annie thought about what Jill said.

Could she be right?

Annie didn't want to be

too scared to ride!

25

Then Annie heard a nicker.

She looked over and saw Surprise

standing at the fence.

She walked over and rubbed the foal
on her soft little nose.
She thought about finding her
as a tiny baby.

Annie also thought about
how much fun it would be
to ride Surprise someday.
Thinking about that
made her feel a little braver.

"I think I will get back on after all,"

she told Jill's mom.

"Hooray!" Meg and Jill cheered.

Annie still felt scared

when she got back on.

Her hands shook as she

picked up the reins.

But Splash did just as she was asked.

Soon Annie was trotting around.

Surprise was trotting along

on the other side of the fence.

Annie smiled at the foal.

"We did it!" She beamed.

PONY POINTERS

tack room: the place
where saddles and
bridles are kept

foal: a baby horse

graze/grazing: what it's
called when horses eat grass

trot: a pace that is a
little faster than a walk

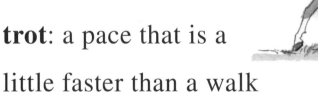